MONSTER HIGH ELECTRIFIED

Voltageous Adventure!

Adapted by Ellie Rose and Gina Gold
Based on the screenplay by Keith Wagner
Illustrated by Jessi Sheron
Designed by Nic Davies

LITTLE, BROWN & COMPANY
LB kids

Illustrations by Jessi Sheron.

Cover design by Elaine Lopez-Levine. Cover illustration by Jessi Sheron.

Little, Brown and Company

Hachette Book Group
1290 Avenue of the Americas, New York, NY 10104
Visit us at lb-kids.com
Visit monsterhigh.com

First Edition: February 2017

LB kids is an imprint of Little, Brown and Company.
The LB kids name and logo are trademarks of Hachette Book Group, Inc.

The publisher is not responsible for websites (or their content) that are not owned by the publisher.

Library of Congress Control Number 2016957626

ISBNs: 978-0-316-54793-2 (pbk.), 978-0-316-54798-7 (ebook)

Printed in the United States of America

CW

10 9 8 7 6 5 4 3 2 1

The illustrations for this book were created digitally. This book was edited by Kara Sargent and designed by Nic Davies. The production was supervised by Rebecca Westall, and the production editor was Jon Reitzel. The text was set in NeutraText BoldAlt, and the display type is House of Terror.

The new Monster High was in full swing. More monsters arrived at the school every day. Frankie Stein was busy in her favorite class—Mad Science! Today, she was working on an electrifying new experiment.

"This is an ultra-high-density direct-current capacitor," she told her ghoulfriends proudly.

The ghouls smiled, but they weren't sure how Frankie's science project worked.

Frankie explained that her science project was a superpowered battery. Using it once could charge their iCoffins for a whole year!

"For the Normies, electricity is everything. This device is really going to change their world for the better!" Frankie said excitedly.

"Why would you want to help Normies?" Moanica D'Kay asked with a groan. "They've never tried to help us."

That night, the ghouls played their favorite game—Truth or Scare!
"What do you dream of doing when we don't have to hide from the Normies?" Draculaura asked Clawdeen.

Clawdeen dreamed of someday opening a salon for Normies and monsters alike. "I'd be the head stylist that makes them all howl *ahooo*!" Clawdeen added with a laugh.

The ghouls thought a salon was a spooktacular idea!

"Why wait for 'someday'?" asked Draculaura. "Let's open it now! We could all work there and get to know the Normies—they'll just think we're in costume!"

Frankie knew the perfect place for the salon! They could use the creeperific power station where she used to hide.

Clawdeen was nervous about opening a salon so soon.

"What if I'm not ready?" she asked.

"You're ready!" her friends reassured her.

Later on, while the ghouls got to work building the new salon, Clawdeen tried to design creeperific outfits. She nearly fainted when Ari Hauntington told her that hundreds of Normies would be at the salon opening that weekend!

"Wait, *this weekend*?" Clawdeen cried.

Clawdeen was nervous that she wouldn't have the designs ready in time. She didn't want to let all her ghoulfriends down.

Meanwhile, Twyla, the shy daughter of the Boogey Man, noticed the Zomboyz acting very strangely. She used her Boogey-powers to hide in the shadows and take photos of them on her iCoffin.

She had to let her class copresident know what was going on!

"Digging tools...electrical equipment?" Frankie said as she scrolled through Twyla's photos. "What could they possibly be up to?"

Frankie asked Twyla to keep following the Zomboyz until this mystery was solved!

A lightning storm was brewing. Big, bright bolts lit up the sky!
"We'd better get back to the school!" Frankie said.
But just as they reached the steps of Monster High, Twyla tripped.
The sky flashed white. Lightning was headed straight for Twyla!
Frankie threw herself on top of Twyla to protect her. She absorbed
all the electricity!

"You saved me, Frankie!" Twyla said. "But are you okay?"

"I'm fine," said Frankie, looking a little dazed. But as she walked away, something odd happened. Jolts of electricity were jumping out of light fixtures and into Frankie's neck bolts! The lightning strike had turned her into an electricity magnet!

That night all the ghouls slept soundly—except Clawdeen.
She was up late at her desk, working on her designs. She
wanted to get them just right, but nothing seemed good enough.
"What are you doing?" asked Draculaura, half asleep.
"I'm just not happy with any of my designs!" Clawdeen cried.
"We have to wow the Normies."

Draculaura let out a yawn.
"Why don't you just bring monster
style to the Normies?" she asked,
already drifting back to sleep.
"Monster style...that's it!"
exclaimed Clawdeen.

The next day, Clawdeen was finally ready to show the ghouls her latest designs—and they loved them!

"I still feel like there's something missing," she told her ghoulfriends.

Then suddenly, Frankie rushed in, looking frazzled.

"I'm sorry I'm late, but I just had this big burst of energy!" Frankie said, talking a mile a minute. "Hey, Clawdeen, those looks are voltageous! Does it sound like I'm talking fast? I'm talking fast aren't I?"

Frankie was supercharged with energy from the lightning!

Frankie touched one of Clawdeen's dresses...and it started to glow! Frankie was *electrifying* Clawdeen's designs!

Clawdeen howled with excitement. "This is what my outfits were missing. A power station deserves electrical fashion!"

Frankie electrified the rest of Clawdeen's outfits. They looked voltageous!

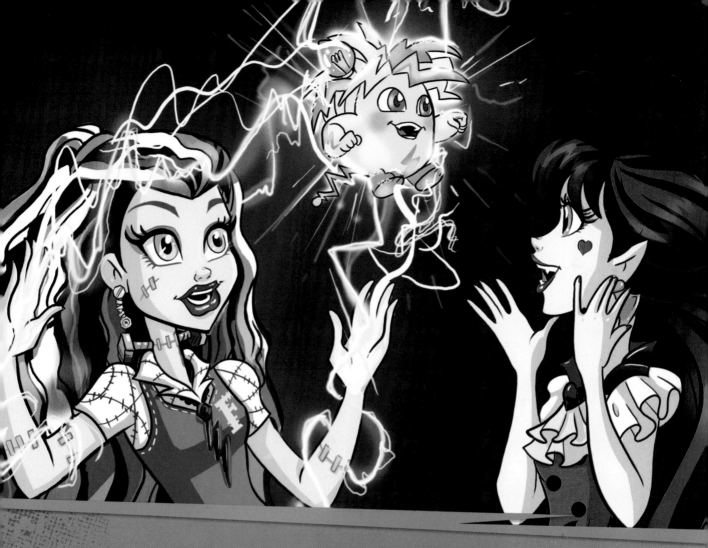

But even after using so much energy, Frankie still felt like
there was a jolt left inside her. She shook her hand—and out flew
a ball of electricity! It bounced around the room. *Znap, znap, znap!*
    The ball finally stopped, and the ghouls saw that it was a little
electric creature!
    "It's adorable! What is it?" asked Draculaura.
    "I guess it's a 'Znap'!" said Frankie.

Meanwhile, Twyla was trailing the Zomboyz to figure out what they were planning. She followed them down a dark tunnel and into a secret cave. Moanica had stolen Frankie's science project and used it to build a giant machine. They were trying to fill it with electricity.

"What are they up to?" Twyla wondered as she hid in the shadows. But this time, the Zomboyz spotted her!

Twyla had figured out Moanica's scheme. Moanica was going to use Frankie's science project to take all the electricity out of the power grid. She was going to ruin the salon opening and Clawdeen's dream!

Twyla was trapped. "I don't care about your friends' little salon or their silly dreams!" Moanica taunted. "Professor Dracula taught us in Humanology class that Normies are afraid of the dark! I'm stealing all the electricity so they'll be in total darkness! The Normies will be terrified!"

Moanica flipped the switch to start up Frankie's science project, but instead of sucking up all the electricity, it released a huge blast of power. The machine exploded! Moanica was furious.

"You Zomboyz are worthless! Now I have to come up with a plan B."

Moanica stormed back into Monster High. She bumped into Frankie, who had been searching for Twyla.

"You wouldn't happen to know where Twyla is, would you?" Frankie asked Moanica suspiciously.

"How should I know where that shadow ghoul likes to creep?" replied Moanica. As Frankie turned to leave, a little spark of electricity shot out from her bolts. Moanica was struck with inspiration.

"Time for plan B," Moanica said as she dialed her iCoffin. "Release the Boogey-girl. She's free to go!"

It was time for the big salon opening! Frankie was headed to the power station when Twyla ran up to her, breathless. Twyla told Frankie about Moanica's secret plot to steal the electricity, scare the Normies, and ruin the salon opening.

Frankie and Twyla had to stop Moanica!

Normies from near and far lined up to get into the new salon. Ari greeted her Normie fans. "I want you all to meet Clawdeen Wolf, up-and-coming style genius!"

"Welcome to...*Fierce!*" Clawdeen announced proudly. The Fierce Salon opening was already a spooktacular success! The Normies loved monster style!

While the opening party raged on, Frankie and Twyla snuck into Moanica's hideout.

"You ruined my science project!" Frankie cried.

"Oh, I'm about to ruin much more than that," Moanica hissed.

Frankie realized what Moanica's real plan was.

"You set Twyla free so she'd lead me here. My science project didn't store enough electricity. You need me to make the machine work!"

Moanica and the Zomboyz captured Frankie and Twyla!

The lights in the Fierce Salon flickered and dimmed. Then electricity shot through the floor, electrifying everything. The lights flickered again and then...darkness! All the Normies screamed!

The salon was pitch black. All of Normie Town went dark one street at a time. Moanica's scheme had worked! Moanica and the Zomboyz burst into the salon through the floor.

"Are you all scared?" she cackled. "Well, you should be! Because monsters and zombies are *real*! And tonight me and my Zomboyz are going out into *your world!*"

The Normies were terrified and ran away!

An opening in the floor appeared beneath the ghouls, and they fell right into Moanica's cave. They rushed over to Frankie. She was in shock!

"We have to get all that energy out of her," Draculaura said.

"And fast, if we're going to stop Moanica," Clawdeen added.

"But she has all of her Zomboyz out there. It will take an army to stop them."

Just then, Znap came bouncing over to Frankie, and that gave Clawdeen an idea!

"Frankie, whatever you did to make Znap, can you do it again?" Clawdeen asked.

Frankie shook her hands as hard as she could—and a bunch of new znaps started flying out!

As the last of the electricity left her body, Frankie felt better.

"Thank you, ghouls. You saved me!" cheered Frankie.

The ghouls rushed outside and saw the Zomboyz running wild through Normie Town!

"We have to stop them, or the Normies will never trust us!" Frankie called to the other ghouls.

"Let's get 'em!" Draculaura cried.

The ghouls and the znaps chased the Zomboyz.

"No!" Moanica groaned. "You're ruining everything!"

The Zomboyz ran away! The znaps disappeared into lights and lampposts and power lines, turning them back on.

"The power's coming back now!" announced Ari.

With all the lights back on, Moanica and the Zomboyz were defeated!

The next day, the ghouls went back to the Fierce Salon. Clawdeen was sad that the opening hadn't gone as planned.

"Let's face it," she cried. "When those Zomboyz popped out of the ground, my dream was as dead as they are. Nobody's going to come back!"

"Look!" Twyla said, pointing out the window. "The Normies thought it was all part of the opening! They loved it. Your salon and monster style are trending all over the Internet!"

"The dream is still alive!" cheered Clawdeen.

"And it's going to be *fierce!*" said Frankie.